A DARK FANTASY LIGHTNING LOVE STORY

SILVERMOON HEAT

VAMPIRE BILLIONAIRES

A.L. SECORD

SILVERMOON

HEAT:

VAMPIRE BILLIONAIRES

A DARK FANTASY LIGHTNING LOVE STORY

WRITTEN BY: A.L. SECORD

DARK FANTASY WEREWOLF MAGIC PUBLISHING

Thank you to my friends and my Sullivan and McEwen family that love and support me. A Big Thank you to: God; Trinity and Tori Secord; Andrey Trushin; Theresa McEwen, Brad Sullivan; Ellen Sullivan; David Fox; Shelley Druet; Annie and Jim Bishop, and Kent and Megs Garlough. Thank you to my fans from all of my heart and soul.

DARK FANTASY WEREWOLF MAGIC PUBLISHING Copyright © 2025
This book is available in eBook, and print formats.

Edited by: APRIL SECORD
Book Cover design by: APRIL SECORD

EBOOK ISBN: 978-1-998151-20-2
PAPERBACK ISBN: 978-1-998151-21-9

First Edition: AUGUST 2025
10 9 8 7 6 5 4 3 2 1

CHAPTER 1

POPLAR POINT ISLAND

Red Poplar Point is actually a small town on the southern part of an island surrounded by the mysterious acres of forest and the dark blue/green foreboding waters of Silvermoon Lake. It's the place I grew up in. Even though I live in a touristy town; this small harbor is home. All people are drawn here like some magnet is bringing them to experience something greater in life. But I've never seen it. I have only heard about it from the tourists of all the strange and exciting paranormal happenings. The ferry comes in three times a day and it brings many worldly people; some of which never go home on that same ship.

The thing that's exciting is the eccentric Silvermoon billionaires on the island and the small town's legend. Red Poplar Point is the actually name of the town but with some strange new laws it's now shortened to

Poplar Point. I think it was a marketing thing. But what makes this place so interesting are the red poplars that actually look crimson and purple. It is a phenomenon that occurs all year round in this semi-tropical area. The legend states the ground and trees were tainted from the blood of the witches tortured and hung. The trees never forgot, nor did the earth. The soil is this mixture which resembles dirt, clay and blood. It makes me feel sick and that is why I will never garden. But the tourists come in boat loads all year round to see such oddities.

The seasons change here from hot to cool but never enough rain to wash away the founder's sins I guess. We just came from the cooler May weather to the beginning of the heatwave of summer. It was also hurricane season which I strongly disliked but what can you do. This was the only home I knew. I have worked at the same retail store for the last fifteen years and met many people coming and going and waiting for a chance to see the unusual billionaires.

But the chances of meeting any of the Silvermoons are rare. I heard it's even rarer to live and tell the tale. Of course this is just hocus pocus small town rumors. I heard they are all exceptionally breathtaking with an air of mystique and danger in their eerie pale blue eyes. Not that I would know until today when I saw him for the first time behind the counter at the small town's library.

There was no way he was just a normal local Librarian. He was too jacked, too handsome. What was he doing in here anyways? I was living at the library on my free time to use the Wi-Fi and linger in that sweet air-conditioning unit. My little bachelor apartment was on the third floor and it was too hot to go home. That's because I was barely making ends meet. But this guy didn't belong here. The only thing that seemed natural about him was his temper over the annoying vending machine that had been around since the dinosaur age and survived the meteor.

I was surprised to see he was just as clumsy as I was, when he spilt his coffee. But once he removed that tight fitting tee shirt it was easy to see his muscles that were carved by the Gods in his golden skin and it was easy to see I was out of my league entirely.

So another day going into night would pass where I would avoid even introducing myself. I would just read another book and secretly steal glances as I turned the page. I didn't mind that the old decrepit Ms. Myrtle that had been there since I was a child had been replaced by this stunning creature.

"I told you he's a Silvermoon. Check out his name tag." I said as I tried to hush while looking at him taking off his shirt again after spilling coffee down it.

"Who cares Lana? You and I both know he's out of our league. These Silvermoons own the town. I bet we have secretly been working for them and never knew it. Man is he ever clumsy but all I can say is yum. Damn I want some of that." My best friend Gina said a little louder and I could feel my cheeks turning red.

"Get in line." I giggle as I look at my best friend and wink.

"Seriously you spend all day and night here. Come have fun with me tonight. I know you're off work tomorrow. Stop staring at this snob and let's go have fun. Don't you want to meet a real guy?"

"He's not a snob and he is real. I think he's just shy that's all. Besides I know where you want to go but it's only Wednesday and there won't be anyone at Mack's tonight." I said rolling my eyes but continued to gaze at the light cascading down his muscular back while he put some books away in front of us.

"Listen, it's supporting local and you never know who will pop up at Mack's. It is the only bowling alley and bar on the island. It's better than wasting your time here. I mean does he even know your name? Has he even said one word to you?" Gina sounded so sarcastic I couldn't even look at her in that moment.

"I think he does. I don't know. I keep checking things out and then returning things. Sometimes he tells me to have a good night or that the library is closing." As I listened to myself I suddenly felt so dumb.

Gina was probably right. But it was still so hot outside and in my apartment; this was my only escape in this small town. It was the one place I knew Gina and I couldn't get kicked out of because no one came to this small town library. Literally no one came here; except us and now him. But he was getting paid to be here.

I bit down on my lip as I watched his muscles flexing as he casually walked shirtless to the water fountain and tried to clean his shirt from the spout.

"Lana stop watching him." Gina stood up to leave but paused as I was silently pleading her to stay.

"Okay I will, but can we please just stay here five more minutes. I am trying to read." I whispered back while I kept looking at the glorious side view of him.

"Oh, so you're telling me you have been reading this whole time we've been here? Wow, Lana I didn't know you were so skillful a reader." Gina said so sarcastically I started getting angry but then gasped as she took my book and I noticed it was upside down the whole time.

"Fine; you caught me. You know I was looking at him. I just can't help it." I said now sheepishly.

"Well duh, I get it. He's gorgeous with his glasses and tight jeans. But I refuse to see you waste your life behind an upside down book and never actually meeting any real people." Gina said loudly and he turned and looked at us both; placing his finger to his full pouting lips.

His eyes enchanted me as he took my breath away when he smiled at us both. His hair was spikey and black and his blue eyes seemed to be looking into my soul just before he broke his gaze to look back at his computer screen again.

"Listen its late and its frigging freezing out. I have to go and you promised you'd walk me home neighbor." Gina said as we both looked at the street lights slowly blinking on and it started to rain.

"Can't we just have five more minutes? It's not that cold out, it's just raining. This is summer for crying out loud. You literally are always cold for crying out loud." I whispered as I returned to holding my book, but this time the right way.

I casually looked over to him again and then this time I saw him look over to me and smile sweetly. He winked just then and I quickly turned to look behind me out the window. When I looked back he was looking at his screen and not smiling.

"Let's go now. I'm tired of being here. It smells funny like someone died in here. And the new Librarian kind of freaks me out. I saw him earlier get so angry over the vending machine and I thought he was going to murder someone if his chocolate bar didn't come out." Gina said in a hush and I started to pack my stuff up.

"Fine, I'm going. Just keep it down okay. You're pretty harsh Gina when I've seen you pounding your fist on that thick plastic window of the vending machine too. I swear that vending machine is diabolical." I said to her in a hush as I looked at the vending machine which seemed to be glowing green neon off the backlight inside it.

"Whatever, let's just get out of here and get pizza. I'm starved." Gina said as she got up and passed the desk without stopping and then I heard his sultry voice.

"Don't you have something to check out?" His sexy deep voice gave me chills as he didn't look up from his computer screen.

"Oh I'm sorry here." Gina said and slammed the magazine down.

I knew it was an accident but Gina was the kind of person that hated to be wrong and in the wrong. So she was mad at herself for forgetting to leave the magazine on the table. But to others Gina didn't seem like a friendly people pleaser at all and she got a little scarier when she was hungry. She was absolutely beautiful and seemed a lot harsher than the truth. But no one ever saw this except me which was unfortunate.

I came up fast behind Gina to check out my book and randomly picked up a movie from the cart to check it out as she waved to me and stormed out of the building.

"I'm sorry she seemed rude. She's actually a lovely person. She gets a little hostile when she is hungry. She gets like mad-hangry when her stomach takes over." I said as I looked over to her outside in the light rain tapping her foot.

"Interesting movie, I hope it works out for you Lana." He said but didn't turn away from the computer screen.

Then I felt my soul die as I read the title of the movie I had just checked out; *'So you have Syphilis; don't be an eighteenth century dickhead get those meds so you can do these three hardcore karma sutra techniques.'* I could feel the blood drain out of my face suddenly.

"Oh I didn't want this one. I am actually a virgin and practicing celibacy. I grabbed the wrong movie by mistake. I want this one." I said as I frantically grabbed another DVD movie from the cart and passed it into his hands.

"Wow, good luck with that." His sexy voice sounded deep and not impressed as my face felt heated.

I looked at the horror of the movie I had just grabbed entitled; *'So your Vagina Smells Funny and is itchy; now what?'*

"Fuck. This isn't what I want to check out either." I said frantically.

"It's okay. All we humans have problems. If you didn't then you wouldn't be so darn cute. You can sort this out tomorrow though. The library is now closed." He said and then walked to the back room without even looking back.

I left the stupid movie on the counter and stomped through the empty hallway kicking the vending machine before I went through the door. I smiled as a chocolate bar came free.

"Finally some good luck." I said as I grabbed the chocolate bar with a wicked grin and ran out the door.

I ran out the doors so fast that I almost missed him in the alley look over to us. He had his black hoodie over his head as he started walking towards the street and to me and Gina.

I turned back to Gina and bumped her by mistake thinking she was further away.

"Jeeze, do you mind?" Gina looked at me strange but I just grinned.

"Sorry Gina, guess what I got though? Something fell out of that horrid machine inside." I shouted as I flashed the cocoa yummy goodness to her hungry green eyes.

"Seriously that's awesome. I must have wasted a good five bucks today trying to get anything but air out of that machine. Finally justice is served." Gina said as she watched me unwrap the candy bar and offered her a piece.

The rain was now coming down harder as my white tee was soaked and I was beginning to look scandalous. Thank goodness no one was out this late as we stood under the street light soaked and sharing a chocolate bar. I took a bite and let the caramel drizzle down the corner of my mouth. I licked my lips and closed my eyes briefly enjoying this moment.

"That looks really good. Do you mind if I have a bite?" The familiar voice made my breath escape as I looked into the pale blue eyes that were directly looking into mine.

All I could do was nod yes as his hand took mine and he took a bite of the chocolate bar from my hands. His lips had gently touched my knuckles as if he was kissing my skin in getting the chocolate and I held my breath as I felt my heart being stolen.

"Hmmm, that sure is good. Here let me get that for you." His eyes seemed to be glowing from the street light.

He took his long slender finger gently wiping up the caramel from the corner of my lips. Then without hesitation, I watched on still in shock as he licked his finger with his long unholy tongue in front of me.

"Oh my name is Luke Silvermoon. I've seen you every day for the last week and I kept forgetting to introduce myself." His alluring voice was mesmerizing as I felt my heart race.

"It's very nice to meet you. This is Lana and I am Gina. Listen I am famished we are going for pizza. We have to go. Catch you another time." Gina said as she pulled me away down the street.

I glanced back but he was suddenly gone and I was angry at myself for not speaking to him. I could still feel his kiss on my skin and all I wanted was more. He had become the victory chocolate that I needed.

"Let's go get pizza at the bowling alley. I have a feeling Mack is there." Gina said in her mockingly dreamy voice that she knew I hated.

"Listen I want someone closer to my age. There has to be more single guys in this small town that just him. Where do thirty year olds go to meet the one?" I said in despair.

"First off there is no such thing as the one. So get that belief out of your head and stop saving yourself for marriage or else you are never going to lose your virginity. Tonight is the night. Let your cherry be free and then you can focus on having fun instead of matrimony."

"I don't know if I can. "

"It's easy. I'll get you drunk and then find you a nice hottie for tonight. It'll be good for you. Break your strict upbringing already. I mean seriously you gotta be the only virgin stripper I know." Gina said and I started to wrap my head around the idea she was right.

"Ex-stripper just like you Gina. I know what you're saying okay but I just wanted my first time to be in the arms of true love." I said and Gina rolled her eyes like I was crazy.

"It doesn't work like that. I only tell you this because you're like a sister to me Lana. I trust you with my life. And I don't want to see you alone like some spinster. Tonight is the night Lana. Your cherry is popped." Gina said and gave me a half hug as she dragged me to the bowling alley.

Maybe I was holding on too tight to the idea there was only one man for me. The more I thought about it the more I wanted to let go and let loose like Gina. I didn't want to stay a virgin forever. Gina might be right after all. She was never lonely and she was happy most of the time. Besides I had never met any nice guys who wanted long term. Maybe I needed a nice guy who was just fun to be with. Tonight would be it. *God I'm scared. I hope Gina gets me more than drunk and I hope the guy I meet is a good kisser and super nice.*

CHAPTER 2

MORALITY IS DRUNK

"The usual Mack and keep it coming. Tonight is the night a cherry is being popped." Gina shouted out as I tried to hush her.

"Not so loud. What if there is someone else here." I said as I looked around and noticed it was empty as per a usual Wednesday night.

"Not tonight pretty ladies. The tourists took off about an hour ago on the last ferry. But I'd like to pledge a hundred bucks to Lana not finding a fellow for tonight." Mack said and laughed heartily.

"I'll see that hundred too. Keep the drinks coming tonight Mack, Lana and I don't have to work tomorrow. Are you listening Lana? You can make a cool two hundred dollars all you have to do is take the bet and lose your cherry tonight." Gina said and giggled with Mack's deep laughter that sounded louder than the radio.

"Fine, keep the drinks flowing Mack. What if there isn't anyone else even here tonight?" I asked as I downed the second round of shots

Mack had finished with us.

"They'll be someone. There has to be or else you're out two hundred dollars dear." Mack said and shook my hand as he grinned and then laughed heartily again.

Meanwhile I started swallowing the next round of shots before grabbing the frothing pitchers of beer and taking them to me and Gina's favorite booth. The booth had a nice sized table and it was secluded enough that we could see out but you had to actually be sitting down at the table to see in. The only thing which was a drawback was it faced the bowling alley and only part of the mini stage for bands. And even with the lights flashing and music booming it was a ghost town in here. I was starting to feel worse about my bet knowing I would have to pay up one third of my paycheck next week. *I'll be living off of ramen noodles again I guess.* I was thinking as Gina clanked my cup and celebrated me.

"Hey ladies you sure look cold. Pizza's on the house if you give me a little show and a jiggle." Mack said through the microphone and announced it through the empty bowling alley and Gina and I smiled to one another.

"Well you're up hot stuff. I flashed the old pervert the last time he wanted to give us free pizza. Besides you're the one who didn't wear a bra today and that white tee of yours is see through. You're practically giving him a free show anyways; we might as well get dinner out of it." Gina said and then laughed as I giggled.

She suddenly grabbed my breast and gave me a motorboat as I giggled.

"Hey knock it off, I'll do it already. Damn I hate it when you know my weakness. I'll do it, but I know you and Mack have something going on even if you won't admit it to me." I giggled as we walked over to the counter but Mack already had seen Gina's face in my breasts and was drooling.

I lifted my shirt with a giant smile and jiggled my obnoxiously large breasts in front of Mack. He hooted and hollered so fantastical I thought I was going to die laughing as Gina carried the pizza over to our table. Then I froze as I hadn't seen the person sitting at the bar watching the whole show. I could feel my cheeks hotter than hell as I seen those strange pale blue eyes that seemed to paralyze me.

It was Luke and I had just flashed him as he dropped his beer and Mack was cheering me on. *Shit. I didn't know he was going to be here. Fucking small towns with locals having nothing better to do, especially when it's the off-season for the tourists.* I thought as I pulled my shirt back down quickly and then turned to follow Gina back in our corner booth.

When I sat back down I noticed Gina had also brought another two pitchers back to the table with our plates and napkins. She was now pouring me another glass and placed it in front of me. I downed it fast as she watched in surprise and then poured me another. I think she could feel my embarrassment as she patted my arm. I could hear Mack teasing Luke for dropping his beer.

"I saw the way he was looking at you. And he wasn't just smiling because of your breasts. He lit up when you were laughing and having fun. So is this why we are drinking faster." Gina said and tried to race me as I finished my glass and poured another.

I didn't speak to her I just nodded and finished another glass before she had even finished her first. Our table was semi facing the lanes; the stage; and a small fraction of the bar. Luke wasn't in my view but his memory was engraved in my mind. He had been just as soaked as we were but he looked like steam was coming off him. He was every bit magmatic wet as he was dry.

"I'm trying to forget this embarrassing day and I need some liquid courage. I took my two weeks of vacation at work. I think I might get away from town for a bit and go to the cottage. I plan on enjoying my time off." I said and smiled before eating a slice.

"Yes, I want you to start enjoying your time off starting tonight." Gina said and giggled and I couldn't help but smile as she then eat a slice.

"Seriously this is the best pizza. Mack out did himself tonight." Gina said as she had surpassed me in inhaling more pizza.

"Agreed, nothing beats free pizza except delicious free pizza." I said and drank some beer between bites.

I knew Gina was seeing Mack even though she wouldn't admit it. All she wanted to do was come here and that was okay with me. I figured with all the money we blew on beer we were keeping this place open on the slow days through the week; which weren't many. Most of the time the bowling alley was so packed it was hard for us to even get a seat at the bar. The busy days we came had a quick beer and then left quickly. But Wednesdays was our day. It was so dead in hear we always had the place to ourselves except Luke's visit tonight. I knew Mack loved us. We were the locales in a small tourist town. I had a love-hate relationship overall for how remote the small town of Red Poplar Point was.

Gina's eyes lit up as Mack delivered another steaming pizza to us. His hair was salt and pepper but you could see his muscles through his blue tee. He was only six years older than us, but we liked to tease him for being older. Mack was quite handsome and with all the women that came through his business I always wondered what tied him to Gina. Gina was stunning but she kept their love secret. I always wondered why because he was successful and sophisticated despite wanting to see our breasts. He was a catch. But she never let me know. All I knew was that he made me feel beautiful when he teased me.

"Here you go my lovely ladies. This is on the house. I hope you enjoy. I'm leaving the box in case you want breakfast too. Gina, can I speak with you after?" Mack said as he placed the empty box on the edge of the table.

He then brought over two more pitchers with a large grin. Gina just smiled and nodded at him. I caught the unspoken chemistry between them both but Gina didn't say a word.

"Lana don't forget to drink up if you're gonna get some cash tomorrow or you'll be paying." Mack said and winked as Gina laughed again.

"I won't let her owe you. She is going home with the next man who comes to our table." Gina grinned so big I couldn't help but smile too as Mack took away our empty pitchers.

Gina finished the last slice of the first pizza and then Mack took the tray away. But Gina didn't look at him while I whispered; *"Thank you Mack."*

Mack gave me a wink and then smiled as he walked away. I watched Gina ogle his firm butt as he walked away and I saw him straighten his back and sway his hips slightly. I smiled because I was now positive Mack knew Gina was checking him out as he left us.

"Gina, why didn't you thank Mack?" I asked her as I poured another glass.

"Because he knows I'm going to thank him later." Gina said and then blushed like I had never seen her blush before.

We started eating like no one was watching and even then there was over half the second pizza left.

"Okay my work wifey that is it for me. I have to go and thank Mack before I leave. Have a good vacation and try and get away from town. You can think about me slaving away at SadZ Department store without you. Remember its two hundred dollars; don't let this liquid courage go to waste. I love you. Call me when you get back." Gina said as she gave me a quick hug and then slipped away to Mack's office through the closed kitchen.

I sat there with one full pitcher of beer and another pitcher almost full. There was so much pizza I didn't know what I was going to do with. I slowly drank my beer as I listened to the music get louder and the lights dim. I was lost in thought before I saw him standing there at the table.

"Excuse me Lana, right? May I join you it looks like we are the only ones left out here? Mack fled to his office with your friend right behind him. My name is Luke Silvermoon I forgot to properly introduce myself." His sultry deep voice gave me goosebumps as I kept thinking about the deal I made.

"Sure I would love some company Gina had to leave." I said as he sat down with the pitcher and glass he brought over.

His eerie blue eyes were driving me crazy as I felt suddenly hot from his direct gaze. *I'm trying to be appropriate but I can't stop looking at his full lips, and his bulging biceps. Even his dimpled chin is so endearing. I can't tell but I think he just bit his lip as he noticed me getting goosebumps through my tight shirt. Good I want him to undress me. I don't know how much more I can control myself. I have never wanted anyone so badly in my life.*

🌾🌾🌾🌾

CHAPTER 3

CLOSING TIME

The way his mouth moved was entrancing as every now and then he licked his lips and his eyes stayed in mine for the most part. I couldn't help but smile as every now and then I caught his eyes look down. He was talking about moving back and how his whole family was conflicted at this time because his Father wanted all his children to be wedded and happy. He was telling me how hard it was to find someone who was kind. I nodded in agreement as I knew all the local guys I went to high school with weren't exactly nice. They wanted short terms flings and I wanted the whole deal and wouldn't be moved.

Until tonight and the bet I made; I hadn't even considered anyone else I wanted to make love to. But Luke was so magnetic I had to drink more beer to distract my mouth from leaning over and kissing those luscious lips of his.

Luke had been talking about how his Father had purchased the library for him to run because of how much he loved books. He had recently moved back to this small town after being in the rushed big city of St. Daemons, off the island.

"It must be nice to escape to St. Daemons from time to time. I wouldn't know. I have never left this small town. Gina and I grew up here. This small town becomes alive during the fall season but is really dead most of the other times during the year. It's crazy to believe that a whole town could be built up off the legend of witches awakening a demon and then being punished. But did you know the real legend is that it wasn't a demon that was risen from the grave but a vampire? It was the very first vampire in the world or so the oldest folk lore whispers through the streets." I said to Luke as his eyes sparkled interest and oozed lust.

I didn't even know why I had told him what the locales whispered. He was a Silvermoon. He probably knew a hell of a lot more than I did just because of his worldliness.

"No I didn't know that. It's simply fascinating the legends or spooky stories passed down to generations, isn't it? Maybe you could show me the haunted cemetery I'm always hearing about. I have the whole month off due to the library building being restored and I would love to hear about this town I always summer in but never know." Luke said and his voice seemed to be oozing deep male charisma driving my failing senses mad.

I couldn't help but linger in his eyes and gaze at his red lips. Even his dimpled chin seemed sexy. His muscles seemed larger than life and all of him seemed to be a golden baked dessert of male bravado that I just wanted to enjoy. He seemed out of place in this small harbor town. There was something about him that really stole your breath away. I listened in pure fascination as he spoke about ancient books as if he had been around during that time. Then he spoke about cars and I seemed to be sitting even closer to him as we drank and laughed about local stories of werewolves and hauntings.

I watched him licking his fingers clean of the pizza sauce and couldn't help but think of devious thoughts and I blushed as he caught me looking at his long tongue and wondering what it felt like to have him lick my entire body.

Then before I knew it we were kissing passionately and our hands were everywhere they shouldn't be in a dimly lit establishment. I was barely able to catch my breath from his soft hands caressing and squeezing me. My hands had gone up and under his shirt in caressing that sun gold skin that I was determined to be next to.

Suddenly I snapped out of my trance and his sultry voice whispering sweetness into my ear that he was kissing. I had the urge to go to the bathroom immediately.

"Luke I'm sorry, can you excuse me?" I asked as he stood up with me and we adjusted clothes.

"Yes, of course." He said and nodded with my lipstick kisses still on his face.

I hadn't realized how drunk I was until I stood up and wobbled to the bathroom. I barely made it to the stall as I flipped my skirt and realized my underwear was missing and then giggled. A few moments later another person came bursting forth with the door crashing against the wall and then opened up my stall to my utter shock as their pants were down.

"Oh my God, I'm sorry Lana. Why are you in the men's washroom?" Luke panicked and shut my door

"I'm not in the men's; you're in the women's." I said and laughed and gulped at seeing his enormous happiness before he realized I was there.

"I swear this is the men's washroom. I know I'm drunk but I couldn't possibly be that drunk. I never get like this. I'm sorry Lana I can't hold it any longer." Luke said as I finished and heard his steady stream in the next stall beside me.

I couldn't help myself but laugh and then he laughed with me as I flushed and leaned on the sink to wash my hands. I laughed even more as I heard him squeak out a fart and then apologize before hearing a flush. *God is he ever cute when he's drunk. I can't believe he's going to be my first.* I thought as he came out rosy cheeked and all smiles.

"I'm sorry I never get this drunk." Luke said as he leaned on the sink too to help him steady himself to wash his hands.

"Me either. Gina and I come here a lot because I think she's dating secretly Mack but usually we just have a few and some pizza and leave." I just had finished saying with a huge grin as he leaned over and kissed me.

Now we were even hungrier for each other and he lifted me to the sink as he kissed me passionately and my legs wrapped around him. I was just as feverishly taking off his shirt as he took off mine. His hands gripped my ass hard in discovering my fleshy bottom without any concealing fabric. Suddenly I was open and my skirt was on the floor as I yanked down his cotton trousers barely concealing his gigantic pulsating desire for me. It was hard to tell in our escalating passion where his flesh and mine had begun and ended. It felt like we were racing across a finish line of love and pain and love. And the victory was the screaming cherish of our voices in winning climaxes to our souls and our sweat clad bodies completely awakened to each other. His lips seemed even more luscious and crimson as I looked over to the mirror and saw him sink his fangs into my neck again and went another round of feverish kisses and movement so high I thought I would pass out from pleasure. *Is this real or am I dreaming. God I don't want to wake up.* I thought as I watched his beautiful taunt muscles in motion with me and watched this mysterious tattoo he had of a dragon on his lower behind. Then we called out again in ecstasy as he leaned on me and I on the mirror; both of us panting and catching our breath.

"Oh Lana, I think I am terribly drunk. I am having such a fun time hanging out with you Lana. You are simply more wonderful than words." Luke whispered as he kissed my ear.

"I have had a great time with you too Luke; even if you shouldn't be in here. I know what you mean about being absurdly drunk. We should probably go home and sleep it off." I whispered back still out of breath as he passed me clothes but I saw him put my thong back into his pocket and smiled.

His glasses were so fogged up it was a wonder how he could even see out of them. He looked so much more alluring and slightly spicier than before. I think I instantly became addicted to him.

"Lana can I walk you home?" His deep voice was even more enchanting.

"Yes that would be nice." I said but meanwhile my heart was skipping still.

❦❦❦❦

CHAPTER 4

CAN I WALK YOU HOME?

Even in the thirteen minutes of walking and holding hands I hung off his every word. He was so funny and mesmerizing that my heart instantly drooped when we were slowly reaching my door. I felt like the heat of our passion hadn't quite disappeared and wondered if he was feeling it too even though he showed no signs of the same desire as before. His hand felt good and warm in mine but if it weren't for his smile I was wondering if I imagined the whole situation at the bowling alley.

I felt like my skin was on fire even as we walked in the rain. I was now soaked again and he was completely drenched. But we were in good spirits. Every now and then we would lean on each other because of us being so ridiculously and deliciously drunk. Now the rain was coming down harder as we stopped on my doorstop and I fiddled with my keys in desperation of his kisses.

"Well it's really coming down now, did you want to come in for a coffee or a tea and warm up?" I said as I just opened and unlocked my front door to my apartment building.

I leaned in close when I asked him and it was too close. We banged heads and laughed as we checked each other for bruises. Then he kissed me so slow I felt my toes curl and my body ache.

Before I knew it we had barely closed the front door to the lobby and we were driven mad again with passion for each other. My clothes had magically melted off and so had his. We feverishly kissed and caressed each other dropping hard to the foyer ceramic floor of my apartment building. I felt like maybe I had become possessed as I rolled him to his back and rode him hard like I was some kind of cowgirl in a fantasy western of my dreams. Then he rolled me back as he kissed me and I felt his fangs pierce my neck as I gasped in pleasure and I called his name over and over in pure delight. His hands and mouth were everywhere and I was completely open to his all as he groaned in a heavy lustful craving. There seemed to be no stopping as we couldn't get enough of each other even when the early dawn's light seemed to peak through the foyer curtains as he laid on top of me passed out temporarily from exhaustion and needing to breathe.

Then I heard his phone ring. It ruined our bliss of heavy breathing and mouthwatering kisses. The ringing was endless; interrupting our magical moments of stolen ecstasy. He hadn't answered his cell phone but I could tell it changed the mood. Then we froze as we heard the loud knocking on the apartment building front door.

"Let me just check babe." Luke whispered breathless as he started to slowly get up and was leaving me naked on the cold dirty floor.

"Please ignore it and come back." I whispered but he just kissed my cheek as I watched him quickly jump into his pants and then peek through the peep hole.

I couldn't believe how open and naked I was as he started putting the rest of his clothes on quickly. He didn't just leave me naked; he had left me wanting more and I was a panting mess still. I looked up to him and he looked down at me straight faced.

"I'm sorry Lana I have to go." Luke said and then I watched the door open and close so quickly in leaving me.

After the silence I became panicked and ran to the large foyer window opening the curtain wide to see where he had gone. I wasn't thinking about anything else as I watched Luke having a disagreement with some beautiful blonde haired woman with pale blue eyes who had looked over to me in disgust. I watched Luke climb into the long fancy black limousine just before the woman gave me a death glare. Luke didn't even look back at me as the elegant car squealed its tires away.

Meanwhile the sun was breaking above the trees and I was left naked in shock still longing after the fancy black car that had sped away taking my dream man with it. *What just happened? Does Luke have a girlfriend?* As I stood there a moment longer still frozen in the window in disbelief the elderly woman who always walked her dog came by. I rolled my eyes and left as soon as I heard; "Good grief you hussy cover up…Can't catch a man if you are always giving the milk away for free."

I gathered my clothes from the lobby floor and walked the walk of shame to the third floor where my apartment was and entered in slowly. The old grandfather clock coo-cooed six times and it seemed to echo off my lonely bachelor walls of my apartment. I was thankful that no one else was up and about this morning as I heard doors opening and closing in the building.

I lingered in the shower and closed my eyes in still feeling his hands and kisses all over my body. *Was I dreaming? How could he have left me so easily? I know I'm beautiful that's the whole reason I still get modeling gigs and can earn extra money. Is it because she is prettier? I didn't even know about her. Luke seemed so great. How could he do this to me? That lady he was with was stunning and very angry. I should have guessed he had someone. He is way too handsome to be single in this small town. I was single because I grew up here and knew all the guys and there was no way I'd date any of them.* A million thoughts went through my head as I just dried off and slipped into bed. My head was now aching as I tried to sleep. I tossed and turned thinking about his pale blue eyes that seemed to glow red as he drank my blood. And I wondered again if I imagined his supernatural existence. *Maybe it was a reflection of the fireplace in the lobby that turned his eyes red and glowing? Wait I don't think the fireplace in the lobby was even on last night. Did Luke really drink my blood? Tomorrow I have to check to see if I have bite marks on my neck and thigh. I'm just so drained.*

❦❦❦❦

CHAPTER 5

STRANGER

I awoke with the worst headache in the world and my whole body was sore; especially my backside from the tile last night. My legs felt like jelly. I didn't bother getting my robe I just walked naked to the fridge and started drinking from the carton of milk. Then I heard someone clear their throat so loud it made my skin crawl.

I looked over and gasped in shock; spraying milk on the floor. The angry beautiful woman from last night was in my house. The air was heavy with the scent of coffee from my favorite mug she was sipping as she sat at the table with an angered and disgusted look on her face. She obviously was unimpressed with me as I turned from her and grabbed my large barbeque apron and put it on to conceal everything she had already seen a million times by now.

"Wwwh…what are you doing here?" I stammered as I could feel myself trembling and my heart quickening.

Somehow she seemed even more terrifying than last night as she glared at me with those piercing pale blue eyes and took another sip of coffee. She reminded me of a lioness keeping her eyes on her prey before she went for the kill shot. *My head hurts so badly.*

"Listen I made myself a coffee while I waited for you to wake up. There is something for that headache of yours on the counter. I left it for you as well as poured you a cup." She spoke and her voice seemed like as if angels could speak; it was that pretty even if she terrified me.

"Thank you but…"

"I wasn't finished speaking. I want you to leave Luke alone. You are just another woman in a long line of woman he has bed with. You don't mean anything to him. He is also engaged. He has been for years now. His mate is wealthy and way above your trashy class of sex in public washrooms. His mate is elegant. She is his perfect match. You aren't even on my class; yet I came here to return some cheap car key he had in his pants pocket from last night. Did you know your door wasn't even locked? Anyways, forget about whatever happened last night between you. I brought him to the train station this morning because his fiancée had just arrived in town. I suggest you keep your home wrecking to the locales." She said and then stormed out slamming the door behind her.

She had left my car key on the table and I was left still shocked as tears started streaming down my face. I was utterly speechless. The air in my small apartment became cold as I sat down at my table and began to sob uncontrollably.

※※※

CHAPTER 6

ESCAPING LIFE

"Holy shit so Luke's engaged? I should have known he was too good to be true. I mean it's not every day you come across a Silvermoon billionaire. I heard the whole family is a bunch of supernaturally beauties. But still Luke seemed too hot to be tied down." Gina said with a shocked expression while she tagged the canned of tomatoes the wrong price.

"I was trying to tie him down. I felt like we were connected spiritually last night. I thought I was more than just fun." I said and Gina hugged me while I started to cry a bit shamelessly in the department store.

"Hey now, it's okay; this was your first time. Of course you think you are connected. You probably feel you are in love. But love doesn't work like that. This is the real world Lana. Forget that prick and chalk it up to at least you lost your virginity and you can brag you scored a

Silvermoon. No one I know has even come close. That's how specific they are about their aristocracy. You guys did do it last night right?" Gina said with raised eyebrows as I wiped my nose off a tissue from my purse.

"Yes, we talked and laughed all night. Then it was so intense we couldn't get enough of each other. I felt like he held my soul as we made love." I said still sobbing as our supervisor came by giving me a look of disapproval.

"You're so lucky it isn't love. He might have just wanted a little fun before he got married to an old hag. Hey sweetie, you don't want to be tied down do you? If it was real love he would have stayed all night and made you a shitty breakfast the next day. You don't want some guy sticking around drooling off you, do you? Think about the freedom you have now. You can still go to your cottage and possibly get laid by all those sexy boaters that zip by on the lake." Gina said as she passed me an envelope then pretended to work as our supervisor walked by again looked disgruntled.

"I don't want anyone else. I don't think I ever want to be with another man again. Guys are just big jerks. What's this?" I said as I looked at the twenties in the envelope.

"Well Mack and I paid up what we owed you from the bet. I hope you can use the money to treat yourself and get away from the town. Who wants to be stuck in this dump of a store if you have vacation time? Go be happy and start enjoying your time off. Don't worry, the next guy you spend the night with you'll probably marry. He'll see how amazing you are, just like I do." Gina said and kissed my cheek while she gave me a big hug again.

My frown grew as I tucked the envelope in my purse while my tears still dripped down my face. Gina was probably right. She had seen a lot of things because she was an ex-stripper.

"I really thought we had a strong connection." I sniffled.

"It was. It was a beer connection and a vodka shooter association. Let him go. There are a million guys in this town who like you a lot. Your ex Ted still wants you bad. He can't control the bulge in his pants every time you're around. Stop going to the library and go to the beach and sun tan. Go enjoy the sun now because the rain is supposed to come in this weekend." Gina said and gave me a wink.

"Okay, I will try and have fun. I'll talk to you later." I said and wiped my eyes and tried to regain compose.

"Okay Baddie; love you." Gina said and gave me another quick hug before I started to leave.

"Love you too BF." I said and left just as our supervisor came by scowling again.

I had just walked out of SadZ Department Store to the parking lot and my car when a gust of wind made me drop my purse. The wind blew my skirt high as I tried to pull it down from embarrassment.

"Nice pink thong. I could help you hold down your dress if you want." I turned as my ex Ted slid his hands down my bodice groping me in the process as his hands rested on my ass.

"Hello Ted, that won't be necessary. The wind is dying down." I said and took his hands in mine and off my backside.

"Well I saw you crying to Gina and thought maybe I could comfort you. You know we never really got a chance after you cheated on me and all." Ted said as he kissed me releasing his hands and placing one on the back of my head so I had to kiss him while his other hand groped my breast.

He leaned in and I felt that bulge in his jeans that Gina was talking about as he pressed into my dress. I paused for one moment in a bad memory of confusing feelings.

"Ted we haven't been anything for the last three years. I thought you were dating the Baker's daughter?" I whispered as he kissed my earlobe and I closed my eyes for a moment imagining Luke was kissing me.

"Come on Baby let me ease your pain. I'm still in love with you." Ted said as he placed my hand on his crotch while he kissed me and slid his hand into the buttons of the top of my dress.

Just then I was fantasizing of kissing Luke and opened my eyes mid-kiss. Suddenly, Luke was there in the parking lot. I looked on in horror at Luke's shocked expression. His fancy black convertible had stopped right beside us. After seeing our public display he squealed his tires as he raced away from me and out of the parking lot. Meanwhile my heart flopped.

"This isn't what I want. You have a girlfriend already." I said and tried to move my head away and my hand off his jeans but he was trying to hold me.

So I swiftly brought my knee hard to his groin making him buckle and drop to the ground.

"Maybe I didn't get the point through to you the first time we broke up. I want nothing to do with you Ted. I'm sorry but this isn't how you could have ever won my heart. And you can't win my heart when you are in love with someone else. That was the real reason we broke up in the first place. You always had a side piece. And I'm not your call girl." I said as he looked at me in hatred now and I didn't care.

"I was doing you a favor Lana. You'll never get anything better Bitch. You know it. You're only getting older and older. And no one wants an aging ex-stripper; no one. Sooner or later those luscious tits of yours will sag to the gutter just like all your dreams of any kind of life that's any better. I'm the best you will ever get Lana. You know it." Ted shouted as I climbed into my car and drove away leaving him still holding his crotch and limping through the parking lot.

I heard his car's loud muffler bang and then watched him speed away in the opposite direction I was going. *Great can this day get any better?* I thought as I watched the clouds start coming in a giant blanket that seemed to block out the sun.

🌾🌾🌾🌾

CHAPTER 7

THE COTTAGE

Immediately, I drove home and started packing for the next two weeks. Gina was right. I just needed to get away from this small town and relax. There would be a million more guys if I wanted them. But right now I just wanted to drive away from my small town and my small problems and escape to my little sanctuary I had bought when my parents died eleven years ago.

After I got a couple of bags, some house plants; and my fat ginger cat in the car; I was off. I drove further and further away from the bowling alley, the diner, and the library. I started thinking about how stupid I was the night before but the cash earned got me gas and groceries for my little home away from home. I looked over to my cat growling as I could hear sweet starlings and other birds in the trees. *Gina has to work and I definitely do not want to run into Ted again or*

Luke for that matter. If I have to be alone than I would rather be at the lake even if it looks like it is getting cloudier by the second. I thought as I watched the sky turning from shades of blue to shades of grey.

While driving I listened to the car radio and sung to songs as I travelled along through the forest. As soon as I reached the little wooden cabin the radio issued a hurricane warning but I didn't care. Even as I unloaded the car, hail the size of golf balls were raining down pelting my back. I sighed heavily as I just made it into the cabin when the rain started pouring and the thunder cracked in the distance.

Quickly I started a fire and got out my candles as the storm wind started sounding like howling outside. My cat Mr. Grumpypants and I were on the couch as the power went out. I lit the candles and started to scratch my ball of fur behind the ears as he purred. Then just as quickly he turned on me and bit my hand hard.

"Mean kitty, bad boy. Why do I love bad boys?" I shouted as my cat jumped away from me and left me in the dim light of the living room.

I started lighting even more candles but stopped as I heard the cat making a really weird growling noise from the entrance way. So I walked over to investigate and froze as I saw the shadow flash in the lightning.

The figure started knocking loudly as I went to the door and opened it. There, as the flash of lightning shot across the sky, was Ted holding a giant bottle of gin.

"What are you doing here Ted?"

"No one embarrasses me like that Lana. This is a small town and everyone was laughing at me when I went in to pay for gas at the station." Ted started shouting as I rolled my eyes even though it was clear he held tears in his eyes.

"No one cares Ted. Literally everyone has their own life. Besides it was a really slow day at the SadZ. There wasn't anyone even in the parking lot except employees on their breaks." I said as he took another swig from the bottle he was holding, while the rain came pouring down.

"Exactly Lana, you made me look like a fool. I demand an apology. And I want you to make it up to me with a kiss." Ted demanded.

"No way, you took my hand earlier and I didn't want you like that. I was temporary enveloped in sadness. Now that I am clear thinking I don't want anything to do with you. Besides your drunk, what makes you think I want to kiss you ever again? Please leave." I said and was about to shout the door as he stopped me from shutting it.

"Lana you are such a cold hearted bitch. No wonder no one wants you. You are so pretty but you don't give a rat's ass about anyone but yourself. Don't you know I seen you with that guy when we were dating? I know you were screwing him while we were going out. You are such a slut. But I will forgive you if you kiss me right now." Ted shouted as he set down his bottle and opened my yellow door wider.

"You're delusional. I don't know what you are talking about and I don't care. Please leave this instant or else I am calling the cops." I said just as he slapped me hard and I fell to the thermal heated stone floor.

I grabbed my sore face and remembered the other reason why Ted and I didn't last long. He was abusive the more he drank and he always assumed I was cheating on him because I was an ex-stripper. It was so stupid that he would be so assuming; as if a dancer couldn't be committed to one person.

"You're going to apologize or else I'm going to make you." Ted slurred as he tried to force my neck into coming closer to kiss his booze soaked lips.

Quickly I grabbed his hand and started pulling his thumb backwards hard as I heard him scream.

"You Bitch I need my hand for work." Ted said as he pushed my head to the entrance wall.

I felt a little trickle down my forehead as I quickly got up and dialed the police station. Then another figure came into the house just before Ted got up and was staggering menacingly to me. The shadowy figure punched out Ted knocking him out.

"Are you okay Lana?" The handsome shadowy figure asked as I looked at his glowing red eyes and fear turned to relief.

Then the power came back on as I watched Luke tie a rope around Ted and prop him up against the entrance wall at the door. Then Luke came over and helped me to my feet. He walked over with me to the kitchen and grabbed an ice pack for my cheek and I just hugged him. As he held me he whispered it was okay. We walked slowly to the couch in silence as I held the ice pack to my cheek.

He took off his shirt and placed it to the cut on my forehead to stop the little blood. And all I could do was just embrace him as we sat on the couch waiting for the police to come.

It wasn't until Ted had actually left that I felt a thousand times better. Luke had made us tea and we just sat there as the storm still whirled around outside. As I sipped on the tea and looked at his pale blue eyes studying mine I just had so many questions whirling around my mind. Like the storms wind the questions where relentless.

"Why didn't you drop off my car key that morning? Your friend wasn't exactly the nicest. You could have told me you were engaged." I said as I could feel my eyes watering.

"I'm not engaged. That friend was my overbearing sister named Tristal. I was so hungover she offered to take your key for me. I had no idea that she told you that lie until after. And then I came to find you and set the record straight instead I found you publicly giving a guy a hand job in the parking lot." Luke said calmly and I was shocked at his lack of emotion.

"I wasn't trying too. Ted was holding my hand to his unimpressive groin. Ted's my obsessive psycho ex. He acts like he owns me still but we haven't been together in three years now." I said rather annoyed with that whole situation.

"Do you think I would invite him here?"

"I don't know Lana. In fact other than us making amazing life changing sex and me being incredibly in-love with you; I don't know anything about you. But my heart would like to believe in yours." Luke said still straight faced and his ruggedness stole my breath away but I turned away.

"I think you should go. Thank you for saving me but I need someone who trusts me. Is that why you came here tonight? You followed Ted's car and was going to confront me?" I asked as I pushed his shirt away.

'No, I came because I heard the shouting and then screaming in-between the lightning and thunder. So I rushed over here to see if you were okay. I was completely shocked to see Ted slap you and that's why I tried to stop his slimy hands from hurting you." Luke said but looked upset.

"Just leave okay. I'm tired and I want to be alone." I said a bit more disappointed than I wanted to be in my lacking strength.

"Fine then; I'm going." Luke said and got up cooler than the ice pack I was holding.

"Just tell me before you go, why would your sister Tristal make up such a horrendous lie about you?" I asked as I started walking him to the front door.

"She lied because she was trying to protect me from getting hurt. I am always meeting really beautiful women who use me for either my body or my fortune. It's been a long time since no one knew I was a Silvermoon and that it didn't matter I was a billionaire. It's been a really long time since I just met someone who is fun and sexy. It's been even longer for me to meet someone who wants more than a one night stand. She was in the car that picked me up from your place that morning and she was the reason why I left so quickly. I wanted to apologize for that night because it was never my intention to move that fast with you. I was just so drawn to you. You listened to me and I felt like you noticed me. Plus I had this indescribable attraction to you the very first moment I heard you swearing at that demonic vending machine." Luke said and I felt my cheeks heat up.

He was just as irresistible as his cheeks went rosy.

"Things have kind of gone astray but I would still like to be friends if you could forgive me?" Luke asked sincerely with his sultry voice and I nodded.

I didn't mean to be smiling but he always brought that sweetness out in me. As I watched him walk down my porch steps I noticed there wasn't any other car in the driveway. Even Ted's car had been impounded. There was only my lonely car.

"Where is your car?" I called out to him.

"I ran here. I tried to get here as fast as I could. My cabin is the house on the hill. We are neighbors. We have been neighbors since you bought this cabin six years ago. I just never had the time to officially meet you. Do you think maybe you'd want to have coffee tomorrow morning?" Luke said in his sexy deep voice and I almost melted as he stood there looking at me for a response.

"Yes, that would be lovely." I said as he gave me a wave and strolled away through the woods up the steep slope and disappeared into the night.

🌲🌲🌲🌲

CHAPTER 8

LOVE AND THE STORM

The rest of that night seemed to be relentless. The wind howled and the cabin creaked. I tossed and turned so much. I couldn't sleep very well and my face still was sore. I kept replaying the last two days in my mind and how incredibly Luke was. His beauty alone kept me awake. He was so sensational I couldn't help but try to live in the memory of his skin and his kisses loving my skin. I had never felt so alive with him. I had never felt like I wanted anyone more in life than when I first saw him at the library.

Usually I could get men but I never had to do anything. Guys were always giving me attention but I never cared for their gazes. But with Luke all I wanted was for him to look at me in desire like he had been. He made me feel special. He made me feel extraordinarily pretty.

I wanted everything with him; the white picket fence and hundreds of kids. I wanted his all and I tried to dream of what it would be like to be his wife. The storm was frightening as I tried to sleep though.

But nothing could keep my thoughts from lingering on Luke's mouth and his perfect kisses. I thought about the corners of his mouth and how eloquently he pronounced words but not in a cruel fashion like he was better than me. He never talked down to me. His blue eyes even puzzled at times only spoke of a sparkling kindness that seemed to radiate off his gaze to me.

Luke had mentioned he was my neighbor staying in the cottage on the hill. But everyone in town knew that old Silvermoon mansion was haunted. Not even the birds sang up there I remembered. While on a jog one morning a couple of years before I had the strange feeling of someone or something watching me so I never jogged on that trail again in the woods.

I switched my thoughts back to Luke's perfect muscular physique. I could see with his black hair and pale blue eyes how anyone could want him. He was stunning. He always wore these form fitted cashmere sweaters that hung snug over his rippling abs.

I wish I had told him my truth. I wanted more than a one night stand too. That was why I was waiting for the perfect guy. It was just too bad my perfect guy came a little late. I had given up on the perfect guy and was on the prowl that night at the bar. I wanted Luke to be tempted that was why I wore that outfit. I wanted him to like what he saw in me. I already had liked him. My growing desire confirmed when he had stumbled into my restroom revealing his large enjoyment for me. *The way his touches seemed to electrify my skin.*

🌱🌱🌱🌱

I awoke to loud knocking and frowned as it interrupted my fantasy of Luke. I stumbled out my room and to the front door in my tiny tee and tiny short-pajama-bottoms without even thinking about who could be out there at this hour of the early morning. In a sleepy haze I opened the door wide as I heard the lightning overhead.

"What is it? Is everything okay?" I asked relieved it was Luke standing there.

"We need cover now. Do you have a cellar?" His voice was deep but seemed to be panicky.

"I have a cellar right here in the living room floor. But it's only a pantry cellar or emergency cellar. I haven't used it in years." I said and yawned as he quickly grabbed my hand and pulled me towards the cellar door.

"Quick we need to get down there immediately." Luke shouted as the wind outside was ear-piercing and I gasped as I saw a giant funnel cloud across the water. Luke lifted the door and gently started to pull me down inside with him. Then I was shocked as Mr. Grumpypants jumped into Luke's arms purring and all three of us went down the small stairs. I had never heard the wind like that.

"You should be safe now. I was worried because you had a rough night last night and I knew you'd be tired. But I had to try to get you up. I just had to make sure you were safe." Luke whispered as he kissed me and I hugged him in kissing him back.

"Thank you Luke and thank you for getting my cat. Mr. Grumpypants never likes anyone enough to be carried like that ever." I said as I petted my mean cat which was still purring in Luke's strong arms.

"I wouldn't say that he likes me too much." Luke just finished saying as the cat hissed and bit him and then jumped to his cat tree in the corner.

I turned on the other light to make the cellar look brighter as we moved and sat on the single quilted bed. There was a little camping cooking stove and tons of canned food. I looked over to Luke admiring the canned meat and smiling.

"I didn't stock the pantry. I had bought this cottage actually from my aunt. I have only been down here maybe three times in the past because of severe storms." I said as I watched him shivering.

"This storm isn't severe. It's the worst. They are calling this storm the biggest hurricane in the last thirty three years." Luke said as we could see the ceiling above rattling.

It really startled me and Luke grabbed my hand. I was grateful he was here with me and Mr. Grumpypants. My cat seemed to care less as he slept in his cat compartment attached to the cat tree.

Luke was shaking even more and I just noticed he was dripping wet.

"Luke you should hang your clothes on that chair to dry out so you won't get sick. I can make us a tea if you want?" I said gently as he nodded and took off his boots.

"Actually I am so worn out. Do you mind if I rest my eyes for a moment?" He said as he started stripping down to his boxer shorts and draping his clothes over a chair.

"Yes, of course." I whispered as he slipped under the quilt and comforter; and suddenly started to softly snore.

Instantly I felt bad because I wondered how long he had been out there struggling with the winds to make sure I was safe. The more and more I listened to his now heavy snoring; the more it made me sleepy. I grabbed the extra sleeping bag off the shelf and made a make shift bed on the floor beside his cot. Then I drifted off.

🌾🌾🌾

Sometime after dawn I heard his sweet deep voice and felt him lift me to the bed.

"Lana you are cold too and the floor is no place for a lady. We can share the bed." He whispered as I nodded to him.

He lay down on his back and I snuggled to his side as he threw his arms around me. We were both shaking as we tried to sleep with the light on and the terrifying wind above us.

�☦☦

I opened my eyes to see Luke's loving gaze into mine and I could feel the blush across my cheeks. I was looking deeply into his eerie beautiful eyes as he whispered; "I am madly in love with you Lana Longfoot. My heart has never beaten for anyone the way it does for you. Will you be mine forever? Can I keep you?"

I was lost in his eyes and whispered back; "I love you too my handsome hero. Yes, I am yours."

"You know I thought we would have more time to get to know each other. But all I know is that you feel like home to me. I don't think I could carry on this boring existence without you." He whispered and then we kissed slowly as the storm crashed above us.

I needed his kisses and comfort as the storm frightened me. The wind howled even louder as the boards above us started moving. Suddenly it felt like we were in this fever dream of motion, loving hands, and wet kisses. We were both crazy for each other and the desire was unstoppable and undeniable with his gargantuan throbbing passion. His kisses were sweeter than all the sweetest flowers in a meadow. And our dance of love reminded me of galloping across a sunny field bareback on the prized stallion. We were frenzied in love and I could feel our eruption spilling over just as his eyes turned red and he gently took a bite from my neck. When he called out in some supernatural language it gave me chills as I called out his name.

Then the cellar roof came off while his fangs were still drinking me in a lovely ecstasy.

"My bride you need to drink from me now if you want to be with me forever. There isn't much time. I can only save one life tonight with the position I am in." He shouted as we both were pelted by the rain and wind and he held me close on the bed.

Then he brought his slashed wrist to my lips and I drank his blood heartily. I felt like I was under some kind of spell or in some kind of lucid dream; and didn't hesitate to drink his crimson essence. But when I did stop drinking his blood; I looked up and could see the galaxy of stars moving through the center of the funnel we were in.

⚜⚜⚜⚜

CHAPTER 9

AWAKEN MY SWEET BRIDE

I listened to the sugary whispers of the words; "Awaken my sweet bride and see with your new vampire eyes."

Softly I open my eyes and looked at my lavish surroundings. I am in this lavish King sized bed and a canopy of heavy red velvet curtains are pulled back for me. I moved my feet over the giant comforter and bedding of fine silks and Egyptian cotton sheets. The floor was this old patterned marble reminding me of the eighteenth century straight from my favorite movie. And the ceiling held an elaborate crystal chandelier. Simply stated it was stunning and it was the fanciest bedroom I had ever been in my entire life.

"Good morning Mrs. Silvermoon. I brought you a drink my love." Luke whispered as I saw him sitting on the bed beside me offering me a large mug decorated in gold.

"Aw, good morning Handsome; where are we? What happened?" I

said as I gently took the thick red drink he had offered but was completely confused.

"This drink will help you this morning. Your head must hurt. I made this special breakfast smoothie just for you." Luke whispered and I gladly drank it all in one shot.

Luke was even dreamier this morning as I looked into his beautiful red glowing eyes. The smoothie he had made me was the best thing I had ever tasted and it left me longing for more.

"Thank you this smoothie was so delicious. I must have been starving. I still kind of feel starving." I said still confused but the drink really did make my headache go away and what also helped me was waking up to his loving eyes.

"It's okay Dearest; I made you another and myself one as well. The roof flew away from your cabin so we are at my family's summer home. Which is now our family ancestral home my beautiful bride." He said so suave that I almost missed the part where he described my cabin's roof flying off.

"The roof? Oh no what happened to Mr. Grumpypants?" I panicked at losing my cat even if he was totally evil.

"He is okay because I was able to save him through your choice. And then I was able to save you. You are a little altered but we can now be together. I could only ever marry another living undead creature such as myself. And I just couldn't let the hurricane take you away. So I turned you; my new ravishing vampire bride." Luke said so charming as he kissed my hand which held the largest diamond wedding ring I had ever seen in my life.

"What so you are telling me the stories are true about Poplar Point and vampires? And I am your bride now?" I said as I was only taken back for one second.

Here was the sexy man of my dreams. He was the very person I lost my virginity to; and a stunningly handsome vampire billionaire but none of that mattered. He wanted forever with me and he was just as crazy in love with me as I was with him.

"Yes my dear; all the stories are true about Red Poplar Point and the witches the townsfolk hung. Centuries and centuries ago; the witches raised my Father from the grave and he brought vengeance to all. But since then us vampires have had a peaceful working relationship with the town's mayor and some humans. And yes my darling you are my bride." Luke said so sweetly I kissed him with all the love in my heart.

"You do remember when we made love and I asked you if you would marry me don't you?" Luke whispered as he kissed my earlobe seductively.

"Not exactly, it's a little fuzzy since I probably had a concussion last night." I smiled and kissed him slowly and felt my fangs elongate.

"Yes, you might have. But you did want me to save a life and I only had enough time to save one life last night. The storm unfortunately took you cabin. I do not regret the decision to wed you my dear. Now we truly can be together forever." Luke said out of breath as I kissed him down his ear to his neck and then sank my fangs into him as he slightly moaned in pleasure.

I was shocked at how lovely he truly was. He saved my cat and then saved me the only way he could. I looked over to the giant ornate mirror on the grand antique dresser. There we were and our eyes matched this red glowing color. I blinked twice and realized my eyes were now the same eerie pale blue eyes just like his. I had changed. I looked as supernaturally beautiful as him. And we looked too good to be real. My wedding ring had such a delicate gold band for such a huge stone and I looked at his matching gold wedding band as I interlocked our fingers.

"Say something my Dear. I am forever your protector; your love."

Luke whispered as I was so turned on by his panting I started to take off his clothes with each ravenous kiss.

"So let me get this right. The legend of the very first vampire ever in the world being raised from the grave in Red Poplar Point is true and he is actually my Father-in-law now? You are a handsome vampire billionaire and my husband? You saved my cat and my life? And I get to have you all to myself for the rest of eternity? Is this all right?" I said as I couldn't stop kissing him even when our drinks fell over to the floor.

"Yes, yes, yes, yes; my darling it is all true." Luke's deep voice sounded raspy as he couldn't control my temptation any more.

"Yes my darling we now share the same last name. Our names are officially '*Silvermoon*'. But we try not to intimidate any of the good people of this small town with our extravagance. I can't wait until you get to meet Dad at dinner. He is dying to meet you." Luke said and chuckled as I rolled my eyes and laughed too.

"Okay my dear Mr. Silvermoon; I can't believe how in love I am with you. Thank you for saving my whole existence." I said as I rolled him through the sheets and we laughed together.

It was obvious that as I had no family other than Mr. Grumpypants; that I was quite happy to be with Luke and a part of his family. Anywhere he was I wanted to be. I didn't have to think twice as we started feverishly kissing each other in our steamy embrace of tangled sheets. He was a perfect dream and a wish come true.

♥The End♥

EPILOGUE

HONEYMOON

"I probably should have asked you this a couple of days ago but Darling Husband of mine; do we kill?" I said and sweetly smiled as we soaked in the sun as we lounged around the ancient Olympic swimming pool and the butler brought us caviar and bloody mary cocktails.

"Oh my Lovely that is pure myth now-a-days. I mean it is true that there are some of us that indulge in the old ways. But you'll see we are very civilized. It really is unnecessary to hurt any living creature anymore. We own the largest blood donor bank in the world and actually pay out for donations quite handsomely. Our wealth is so great we could go on absolute mindless shopping sprees and never even make a dent in our bank accounts. That was why I bought the library and took the librarian position. I love books and just wanted a fun experience. Little did I know that I would have a heinous demon co-worker trying to steal my money and not give up the goods." Luke said as he cheers my crystal glass.

"Yes, that demonic vending machine has been stealing people's money for years." I laughed as I sipped on my cocktail which had real 'O' negative blood in it.

"You were the first human I had ever turned; the first person I had ever drained. But I had to save you from the hurricane that was going to rip you apart." Luke said as he frowned and looked at two swans that had landed on the lake across from our glorious view.

"Actually I am quite thankful my dear husband. You have already granted my biggest wish. You have given me the best happily ever after for all of eternity. I think I first fell in love with you when you stumbled into my restroom." I said and giggled as he smiled and blushed.

"I'm still positive it was the men's and you weren't supposed to be in there." Luke said and I rolled my eyes but grinned.

"I know I have told you about falling in love with you when I first saw you swearing and kicking the vending machine. But I had forgotten how adorable you were when you kept checking out the wrong movies." He laughed and I laughed too.

"Hey that wasn't my fault. Do you know how hard it was for me to even be able to talk to you? That was not my finest time may I add. I would say that whole day was a disaster but if it had happened any other way we probably wouldn't be laying on sofa's and tanning by the pool. It ended up being exactly what I never knew I needed and was missing in my life." I said and moved over to his sofa and kissed him as he embraced me.

He squeezed me and then moved so I could lay with him as he held me. He sighed deeply and I knew how he felt. The last couple of days had been pure heaven. I glanced over to the bottle of wine Gina and Mack had given us as a wedding gift and it made me smile even warmer as I closed my eyes in his strong arms.

"We have two more weeks of bliss my lovely bride and then I will introduce you to the rest of the Silvermoon clan. Don't worry they will love you. I already told Tristal about you and she is super thrilled." Luke said as I looked at him a little puzzled.

"Really? Tristal is thrilled?" I said with a grin and he shrugged and smiled sheepishly.

"Okay well mostly. What can I say? My sister is a bit of a hard-ass when it comes to the family. But now she knows you aren't going to break my soul and stake my heart; so she's actually looking forward to seeing you on better terms and becoming friends." Luke said and smiled as I tickled him a little and he laughed.

"You mean this lovely muscular chest that has an undead heart beating wildly for me?" I said as I rubbed my hands across his muscular pecs and down to his abs but moved back up to his heart.

"You have my matching undead heart already and I promise to be good to your heart too my Darling." I whispered as he started kissing me so deep and loving I felt like I was going to fly right up into the clouds.

🌲🌲🌲🌲

ACKNOWLEDGMENTS

I would really like to express my sincere gratitude to; The Universe, my fans, family, and friends. Its fine people like you that give struggling authors a chance. Thank you again!

I would also like to thank my mechanics and my friends Eric Heldman and Jay Flowers at Good Year Obsentia, in Quinte West, Ontario. Thank you for always being great friends and taking care of my car. I am so appreciative that you are lights in the world and practice random acts of kindness every day. Thank you again for not suing me for killing off your characters in future novels! Their website is here if you want some kind individuals helping you with your auto needs and are in the Quinte West Area: https://www.trentontire.ca/

Thank you for reading!   I really hope you have liked my book. Please add a short review and let me know what you thought!

And always let your light shine bright!

ABOUT THE AUTHOR

A.L. Secord is a pen name for the author APRIL SECORD. She enjoys many genres. But she is most passionate about Dark Fantasy Romance. She loves learning new things, and occasionally burning food for the ones she loves. She is an author, a proud mother, and an avid adventurer of the unknown; on her many pursuits for greater happiness and Bigfoot.

A DARK FANTASY LIGHTNING LOVE STORY

SILVERMOON PASSION

VAMPIRE BILLIONAIRES

A.L. SECORD

BOOK TWO

A DARK FANTASY HORROR ROMANCE

BLOOD MOON KISSES

ENEMIES TO LOVERS

A.L. SECORD

A DARK FANTASY ROMANCE

THE HOUSE WINS

APOCALYPTIC FRIENDS TO LOVERS

A.L. SECORD

A CHRISTMAS DARK FANTASY ROMANCE

FOREST LOVE

BROKEN VAMPIRE PRINCE

A.L. SECORD

A DARK FANTASY ANTI-HERO ROMANCE NOVEL

THE LAST KING

EVIL TASTES GOOD

A.L. SECORD

__Other books by A.L.SECORD__: